PIRATE SCHOOL

Attack on the High Seas!

by Brian James
illustrated by Jennifer Zivoin

Grosset & Dunlap

For my brother Aaron.—BJ

For my husband, Rome, my shipmate
through all of life's tangles and knots.— JZ

GROSSET & DUNLAP
Published by the Penguin Group
Penguin Group (USA) Inc., 375 Hudson Street, New York, New York 10014, U.S.A.
Penguin Group (Canada), 90 Eglinton Avenue East, Suite 700, Toronto,
Ontario, Canada M4P 2Y3
(a division of Pearson Penguin Canada Inc.)
Penguin Books Ltd, 80 Strand, London WC2R 0RL, England
Penguin Ireland, 25 St Stephen's Green, Dublin 2, Ireland
(a division of Penguin Books Ltd)
Penguin Group (Australia), 250 Camberwell Road, Camberwell, Victoria 3124,
Australia (a division of Pearson Australia Group Pty Ltd)
Penguin Books India Pvt Ltd, 11 Community Centre, Panchsheel Park,
New Delhi - 110 017, India
Penguin Group (NZ), 67 Apollo Drive, Rosedale, North Shore 0745, Auckland, New Zealand
(a division of Pearson New Zealand Ltd)
Penguin Books (South Africa) (Pty) Ltd, 24 Sturdee Avenue, Rosebank,
Johannesburg 2196, South Africa

Penguin Books Ltd, Registered Offices:
80 Strand, London WC2R 0RL, England

Library of Congress Control Number: 2007007359

ISBN 978-0-448-44645-5   10 9 8 7 6 5 4 3 2 1

Chapter 1
Gruesome Grub!

"Shiver me timbers! What's that smell?" I asked Gary as we walked into the mess hall. I pinched my nose as tight as I could.

I've lived on pirate ships like the *Sea Rat* my whole life, so I'm used to stinky smells. But the stink that I smelled coming from the kitchen was worse than any other.

Gary wiped the sniffles from his nose and took a big sniff.

Then he sneezed!

Gary was my best bunkmate at Pirate School. He had come to the *Sea Rat* from another ship to learn how to be a pirate, just like me and the rest of our friends.

"I can't smell anything," Gary said. He

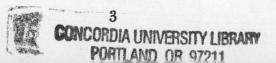

was still stuffed up from a cold he caught in the last storm. We were the ship's lookouts, and we got soaked. Then Gary got sickish.

"Then ye be the luckiest matey aboard," I told him.

I looked around the mess hall. The place was filled with some of the rowdiest pirates the seas had ever known. Some had big scars across their faces and others wore eye patches to make them look scary. But they didn't scare Gary or me. That's because those pirates were our shipmates. And shipmates aren't allowed to scare other shipmates—that's a pirate rule.

I saw Inna right away. She was easy to spot. That's because Inna was the only pirate wearing a pretty dress. She's also the only pirate I know who brushes her hair. But instead of wearing her bandana around her head, Inna had it tied around her mouth and nose. I guess she was trying to block the smell, too.

"Ahoy!" I said. Then I asked her what stunk so bad.

4

Inna lifted the corner of her bandana and stuck out her tongue. "Breakfast!" she said, and pointed toward the kitchen.

I saw our friends Aaron and Vicky standing at the stove. They were both wearing matching aprons. They're twins, so they always wear matching things. And they look alike, too. They have the same dark eyes and same black hair. Only Vicky has long hair and Aaron has short hair.

"Ahoy, Pete!" Vicky said when she saw me.

"Ahoy right back," I said.

Aaron was tossing something slimy into a giant pot while Vicky stirred. Neither of them seemed to mind the terrible smell.

"Arrr! What in the name of the seven seas are you guys doing?" I asked.

"Cooking!" Vicky said with a smile.

"Aye? Are you sure you're doing it right?" I asked.

"Aye!" Aaron answered. "It's an old family recipe—sea slug cereal. It's our favorite food. Captain Stinky Beard said we could make it because we saved the ship in the storm."

I looked around and saw the other pirates eating bread and jam. I loved bread and jam! "Arrr, but what about them?" I asked.

Vicky said it was a special treat just for us pirate kids. Then she dipped the spoon into the pot and took it out. I saw a slug on the spoon and felt a little greenish.

Vicky took a little taste and rubbed her tummy. "Mmm-mmm! It's ready! You're just in time."

"I am?" I asked, wrinkling up my nose. I was beginning to wish I'd been late.

"Aye! Grab a bowl and get some grub," Vicky said.

I took a bowl and brought it over. Vicky scooped out some cereal and plopped it in. I did my best not to show that I was grossed out.

"Say when," Vicky said.

"When!" I said right away.

"Avast! That's all?" Aaron said when

he saw how little I'd taken. "I'm going to gobble up five times that much!"

"Don't be such a greedy guts!" Vicky shouted at him.

"Arrr. That's okay," I said. "Ye cooked it, you should take as much as you want."

"Aye, it's only fair!" Inna said, holding her hand over her bowl after Vicky put the tiniest of tiny scoops in it. Then Vicky asked her why she was wearing her bandana like a scarf.

"Um . . . germs," Inna said, pointing at Gary's sniffling nose. Inna was always the best at thinking up ways to get out of trouble.

Gary was next. He took a peek at the sea slugs and gulped. Even if he couldn't smell it, he could see that it looked yucky. "Aye, no more for me!" he said. "I'd probably just spill it on the way to the table," he added to be nice. And it worked, too, because Gary is the clumsiest pirate kid any of us have ever met. So Aaron and Vicky had no reason to think he was fibbing.

We all sat at the table. All the other pirates took one whiff and moved a little bit away. Then they started to leave one by one until we were the only ones left in the mess hall.

I watched the sea slugs squirming around on my spoon. I had to close my eyes before taking a bite. I was surprised to find out it didn't taste as bad as it smelled. Believe it or not, it tasted a hundred million times WORSE!

"Yum," I said, trying not to gag.

Inna brought her spoon up and lifted her scarf. She made a face like she was taking medicine, and then she took a bite. Her eyes opened so wide as she swallowed that I thought they were going to pop right out of her head.

"Mmm," she squeaked.

"Aye? You like it?" Vicky asked.

I nodded.

Inna nodded, too. "But it could use a little cinnamon," she said. Then she raced over to the cupboard and brought back the cinnamon. She scooped ten spoonfuls into her bowl.

When I looked over at Gary, I couldn't believe my eyes.

He'd already finished everything in his bowl.

Then I looked at the floor by his chair and saw a puddle of sea slug cereal. Gary glanced over at me and gave me the *shhhhh!* sign.

"Yo ho ho! This sure is some good slop," Aaron said, shoveling his mouth full of the gruesome grub.

"Aye!" Vicky said, slurping up another spoonful. Most of the time, Vicky and Aaron argued about everything. But they agreed when it came to their family recipe.

Just then, Rotten Tooth stormed into the mess hall. Rotten Tooth was not only the ugliest pirate on the *Sea Rat*, he was also the meanest. He had green hair and green teeth and mostly yelled a lot. Plus he was our teacher, and he didn't like us one bit. But I'd never been happier to see him!

"Arrr! What are ye lazy sprogs doing in here?" he growled. "Ye be late for Pirate School!"

"Avast, we were just finishing," I said.

"Ye better be! Any pirate not on deck in the shake of a whale's tail will be on kitchen duty," Rotten Tooth warned. He looked around and saw the slop spilled all over the place. Then he sniffed and made a face like we do when we smell his breath. "Arrr! And by the stink of it, kitchen duty is about the worst place on the ship today."

I sprang up from my seat and tossed my bowl onto the pile of other dirty dishes. I wasn't going to miss my only chance to get out of eating the rest of my breakfast.

Chapter 2
All Hands on Deck

"Arrr! I wonder what Rotten Tooth is going to make us do today?" I whispered to Inna and Gary. I had to whisper it real quiet, too, because Rotten Tooth could hear *everything*!

"Arrr! I hope it won't be anything soggy!" Gary said.

Then he sniffed, sniffed, and sneezed again. He sneezed so hard, he blew his glasses right off his nose.

"I don't care what it is as long as it's real pirate stuff," I said. I want to be the captain of my own ship when I grow up, so I need to know everything about pirating. But most of the time Rotten Tooth didn't teach us any real pirate things. He thought we should all be deckhands.

Lucky for us, he wasn't the boss of the ship. Captain Stinky Beard was, and he thought we were shipshape pirate kids.

"ARRR! Fall in, ye scurvy pups!" Rotten Tooth said with a snarl.

Inna, Gary, and I rushed over and stood in a straight line. Then we gave Rotten Tooth a salute. Even if he was as rotten as his name, he was still our teacher and the ship's first mate, so we had to give him a salute. That's part of the pirate code.

Rotten Tooth paced in front of us. The *Sea Rat* shook as he stomped his boots. "Where be those other two pollywogs?" he asked.

I shook my head.

Inna shrugged her shoulders.

And Gary sneezed.

I thought for sure Aaron and Vicky were going to get stuck with kitchen duty. But just then we heard footsteps. Aaron and Vicky burst through the door and ran over to us, their mouths still full with one last bite of sea slug cereal.

"Arrr! Ye sea dogs made it just in time,"
Rotten Tooth said. "Ye be lucky I'm a nice
pirate."

"Aye, nice and stinky," Vicky whispered
to me.

I had to cover my mouth to hold in my
giggle.

"Arrr! I don't have time for ye mangy
litter today," Rotten Tooth mumbled. "The
Sea Rat is being chased by another ship. A
rival pirate ship named the *Filthy Sails*."

We all gulped!

The *Filthy Sails* was the most dreaded pirate ship there was. Grown-up pirates were always telling scary stories about the ship to us pirate kids. They said it sank every ship it attacked and made the crew walk the plank. Even the kids! And its captain, Captain Fish Face, was even meaner than Rotten Tooth. And uglier, too! He had whiskers like a catfish, and his face was all squished up like a fish.

"Are they going to attack?" Inna asked.

I could tell she was a little scared because her hand was shaking. But I wasn't scared. Captain Stinky Beard could outsmart that fish-faced captain.

"Can we help fight them off?" I asked.

"AYE! We'll sink their ship lickity-split!" Aaron shouted.

Rotten Tooth waved his arms in the air. "Quiet," he growled. "The only thing ye will be doing is keeping out of the way!"

We all moaned and groaned. It sounded like Rotten Tooth was going to make us do chores, like swabbing the deck or emptying the fish-gut tank. It wasn't fair. We were part of the crew, too.

I stepped forward and raised my hand. "But Captain Stinky Beard said you had to teach us more pirate stuff."

"Arrr! I'll be teaching ye all right," he barked. "But the cap'n never said *what* I had to teach you. Ye little shipmates think pirating is all swashbuckling and treasure?"

"Aye! And good grub, too!" Aaron said.

"Aye! And pretty jewelry!" Inna said, and proudly showed us her shiny necklace.

Rotten Tooth let out a fearsome laugh. He laughed so loud, I saw the sails puff up! "Captain Stinky Beard was right about one thing, ye really do have a lot to learn!"

I was confused. "Blimey! Isn't that the point of Pirate School?" I asked.

"AYE!" Rotten Tooth roared. "And I'm the teacher, so that means I decide what ye learn and when. And I'll be making sure ye learn all the boring stuff first. And I'll also be sure to give ye so much homework that I won't have to hear a peep out of any of you!"

Boring stuff? Homework? Pirate School wasn't sounding like so much fun anymore.

Chapter 3
Knot So Much Fun!

Inna stretched out her arms. Then she picked up the rope with only the tips of her fingers. "Eww! This rope is all slippery and slimy," she said.

"Aye, and it looks like a snake, too!" Gary said.

"YUCK!" Inna screamed and dropped the rope back on the deck. Then she gave Gary a mean look. "Why did you have to bring up snakes? I hate snakes!"

Gary covered his mouth with both hands. "Sorry."

"Arrr! Don't be such a scallywag! It's just a silly rope," Aaron said. "And the sooner we learn how to tie all those knots, the sooner we'll be able to join in the battle." Then he picked up the rope with both hands. He started swinging it around, pretending to fight off the crew of the *Filthy Sails*.

"Scallywag yourself!" Inna shouted. "Besides, there might not even be a battle. And even if there is, we just have to feed them your sea slug cereal and they'll run off on their own."

Vicky spun around. She folded her arms and lifted her chin high in the air. "Arrr! What's wrong with our sea slug cereal?" she asked.

"Everything's wrong with it!" Inna yelled. "It tastes like someone already ate it once, and it smells that way, too!"

Vicky put her hands on her hips and huffed. "Aye? Well it's better than those fish eggs you made us eat that one time!"

"Those fish eggs are called *caviar*," Inna hollered.

"Well I call them icky sticky, so there!" Vicky hollered right back.

I didn't like all my best mates being so grumpy. I took off my pirate hat and waved it around to get their attention. "Blimey! What's ruffled your sails?" I asked.

They all stopped to look at me.

"KNOTS!" they yelled, except Gary, who sneezed instead.

After Rotten Tooth had shown us how to tie a few knots, he had left. He had told us we had to practice knot tying for the whole entire day. Plus he had said we wouldn't learn anything else until we mastered all three knots he'd taught us. He'd shown us how to tie a Fisherman's Bend knot, a Bowline knot, and even a Sheepshank Man-o'-War knot. And that's the hardest knot there is!

"What's wrong with tying knots?" I asked.

"It's boring!" Vicky shouted.

"And slimy!" Inna added.

"And it's not swashbuckling," Aaron yelled.

"Aye! And it makes my feet all tied up," Gary mumbled, looking down at where his feet were tangled in the rope.

"But tying knots is an important part of sailing," I said. "And everyone knows pirates are the best sailors on the sea. If we're going to be the best pirates, we need to learn all of these knots."

Inna put her finger up to her mouth. Gary scratched his head. Aaron and Vicky squinted their eyes. I knew what those looks meant. It meant they were all thinking very hard.

"Pete might be right," Vicky finally said. "Knots hold sails to the mast and keep ships from floating away from the dock."

"Oh, barnacles!" Aaron moaned. "Any knot can do that. Why do we have learn so many different kinds?"

"Not any knot," Vicky argued. "Remember on our last ship when you made a bunny-ears knot to tie our dinghy to the pier?"

Aaron's cheeks turned red. He had a guilty look on his face. "Um . . . maybe," he said.

"Arrr! I remember! Our boat floated away, and we had to swim after it!" Vicky shouted.

Aaron put his head down. "Oh yeah, I remember."

"I know!" I said excitedly. I had a plan. "We'll do such a good job doing this that Rotten Face will have no choice but to let us help defend the ship!"

My friends thought some more.

"Aye aye!" Vicky, Gary, and Aaron agreed.

Inna wasn't so sure. The rope still looked like a soggy snake.

"I've got an idea!" I said. "You can practice your knots with the ribbon from your dress."

Inna smiled. "Aye! I can. And my ribbon's not even gross because it's the prettiest one I have."

"That's the spirit, matey!" I said.

Then we all formed a circle. We put our hands in the center and gave our pirate cheer. "SWASHBUCKLING, SAILING, FINDING TREASURE, TOO. BECOMING PIRATES IS WHAT WE WANT TO DO!"

Chapter 4
Tangled Up Forever!

"Arrr! This Sheepshank Man-o'-War knot is impossible!" I said to my friends.

We were all able to finish the first two knots, even Gary. But none of us was able to do the last one. There were too many loops and twists.

I tried it a thousand times. I wasn't sure it was exactly a thousand. I lost count, but one thousand sounded about right.

"Aye, we're never going to finish," Gary said.

"Quit bellyaching!" Aaron said. "It's not that hard. I could do it with my eyes closed."

"Then how come you haven't done it yet?" Vicky asked him. She didn't like it one bit when Aaron bragged. And Aaron *always* bragged!

"Because I didn't want to," Aaron answered.

"You mean because you couldn't," Vicky corrected him.

"I could if I wanted to," Aaron said.

"Fibber!" Vicky said. "Prove it!"

"Fine! Gangway!" Aaron said, and grabbed the rope. He squinted his eyes and stuck out his tongue. That meant he was trying really hard. It sure was one silly face. I started laughing my head off. "What's so funny?" Aaron asked.

"It looks like you're trying to go to the bathroom." I giggled. Soon the rest of my friends were laughing, too. But not Aaron. He got a little mad. His face turned red, and he squinted even more. That made us giggle louder. Then he made the last loop and pulled both ends of the rope.

"Ta-da!" he said proudly, and lifted the rope to show us.

Only it wasn't really a *ta-da*, because

both of his hands were caught in the rope. That's when we all fell to the deck from laughing so hard.

"Ahoy! You little shipmates seem to be having fun!" a voice boomed behind us. It was Captain Stinky Beard, and he had a big smile on his face.

"Ahoy right back!" I said, and gave him a pirate salute.

Captain Stinky Beard saluted back. Then he took a look at the knots in our practice rope and the ones in Inna's ribbon. He nodded his head and said, "Ye sailors have been working hard at these. It looks to me like you've done a fine job."

"Aye?" we asked.

"Aye!" Captain Stinky Beard said.

"But Cap'n? Shouldn't we be helping the rest of crew get ready in case we're attacked?" Vicky asked.

"Aye!" Aaron said. "All this knot tying is a waste of time!"

"Arrr! Knot tying is very, very important," Captain Stinky Beard told us.

I smiled. "That's what I said," I whispered to my friends.

"Besides," the captain added, "there's been no sign of the *Filthy Sails* all day! They must've heard about our brave little pirates."

"Aye!" we said proudly. We were all smiling, too, because as much as pirates like adventure, no pirate likes to be attacked. But our smiles disappeared when Captain Stinky Beard looked at our practice ropes again and frowned.

"Are these supposed to be Sheepshank Man-o'-War knots?" he asked.

We put our heads down and nodded. They didn't look much like knots. They looked more like messes. We thought the captain would be disappointed. But when I peeked up, he didn't look disappointed.

"Hmm, not bad," he said. "Rotten Tooth must have a lot of faith in ye mates to teach you such a hard knot."

"Aye, Cap'n!" Rotten Tooth bellowed. It was the end of the day, and he was coming back to check on us. He put one of his big hands on my shoulder and the other on Inna's. Then he smiled real wide. "I got a whole ocean of faith in 'em!" he said.

I looked over at Aaron and rolled my eyes.

Aaron rolled his, too.

Rotten Tooth was always pretending he liked us in front of the captain. But as soon as Captain Stinky Beard left, so did Rotten Tooth's smile. He leaned in real close to us. We had to hold our noses because of his stinky breath. "Arrr! I got faith that ye will never, ever figure it out!"

I folded my arms and stomped my foot. "Arrr! We'll figure it out," I told him.

Rotten Tooth roared with laughter. "Mayhaps, me little buckoes. But it took me two years to learn how to tie and untie that knot," he said, holding up five fingers.

"TWO YEARS!" we all yelled at once.

Two years was forever. I was already nine and three-quarters years old. In two years, I'd be way into my tens! I couldn't waste all that time learning one knot.

"How are we ever supposed to learn anything new?" I asked.

Rotten Tooth scratched the two pointy ends of his beard. "Arrr, I suppose ye better keep practicing for homework."

We all groaned as Rotten Tooth cut each of us a small piece of rope to take belowdecks. But I wasn't going to let

Rotten Head stop me from being a real pirate. I'd show him! Even if it took all night, I was going to learn the Sheepshank Man-o'-War!

Chapter 5
Ships Ahoy!

The next morning, I was sitting on my bunk as the sun was waking up. The ship was quiet except for Inna's snoring and Gary's sleepy sniffling. Aaron and Vicky were asleep in their bunks, too.

They were all tuckered out from doing homework the night before. We had practiced and practiced until our fingers were sore. But still, not even one of us had been able to get that knot to tie the right way.

I didn't want to spend another day working on it. So I reached under my pillow and took out my practice rope. I made four loops like Rotten Tooth had shown us. That was the easy part. Then came the hard part. I had to pull the center loops back through the other loops and turn them from front to back. It made my brain dizzy just thinking about it. And when I was done, my finger was caught in one of the loops. I had to start all over again.

I made a growly noise.

"Knots are not fun," I mumbled.

I made four more loops and was about to try the twisty-turning thing when I saw something out of the porthole. It looked like it might be another ship. Maybe the *Filthy Sails* was coming for us after all.

I pressed my face up to the glass and took a longer peek. I didn't see anything.

I peeked to the front side.

Then I peeked to the back side.

I only saw waves. It must have been my imagination.

When I peeked at my lap side, I couldn't believe what I saw! While I was doing all that peeking, I'd tied a perfect Sheepshank Man-o'-War knot! I forgot all about the ship I thought I saw.

"Avast! I did it! I did it!" I shouted.

Vicky woke up first. She sat up on her bunk and rubbed her eyes. I held up my rope for her to see. Then Vicky started clapping and shouting, too. "Pete did it! He did it!" she yelled and banged on the bunk above her where Aaron was still sleeping.

Aaron sat up. "Arrr! I told you it wasn't impossible," he said.

Vicky didn't answer him. She just stuck her tongue out instead. Then she got up and raced over to my bunk. Gary's bunk was under mine. Vicky had to step on his to climb up. By accident, she stepped on his hand. Gary woke up.

"Good morning, sleepyhead," Vicky said.
"Aye-aye-AH-CHOO!" Gary said back.

I poked my head over the side and showed him my knot.

"Blimey!" he said. "Good job, Pete!"

"Thanks, matey!" I said.

Finally, Inna pulled back the pink curtain around her bed. "What's all the racket? I'm trying to get my beauty sleep," she said.

But when I told her what I'd done, she wasn't grumpy anymore.

She gave me a thumbs-up. "Maybe now you can show all of us?" she asked.

"Aye! Rotten Tooth showed us too fast. You could show us in slower motion," Vicky said.

I made my face into a pout. Then I scratched my head. "Aye. I wish I could. But I was looking out the window when I tied it," I told them. "I'm not sure I could show myself."

"Why in the name of the *Sea Rat* would you be looking out the window?" Vicky asked.

"Aye. You're the one who says we

need to pay attention when it comes to important stuff like homework," Inna said.

"Aye aye. But my brain was all dizzy, and I thought I saw a ship," I said.

"Arrr! You mean like that ship?" Gary said, pointing out to sea.

I spun around. Outside the porthole was a ship. And not just any ship, it was another pirate ship. "Sink me!" I said. "It's the *Filthy Sails*!"

My friends all made a really loud triple gulp!

"We need to get on deck and help the crew!" I shouted.

"Aye!" Aaron agreed. "We'll teach Fish Face not to attack our ship."

"Aye aye!" Inna, Vicky, and Gary said.

We were just about to run out of our room when Rotten Tooth came in. "Arrr! Where do ye pollywogs think you're going?" he asked.

"To show those mean pirates who the boss of the sea is, that's where!" Aaron answered.

"Arrr! A high seas attack is no place for kiddies," Rotten Tooth growled. "Ye'll weigh anchor here and work on your lesson."

"But Pete already did," Inna said. She held up my rope and waved it in front of Rotten Tooth.

"ARRR! Then practice untying it and re-tying it! And that's an order!" he yelled, and slammed the door.

We all moaned and grumbled. But orders were orders even if they weren't fair! It was the first battle since we'd come to Pirate School, and we were all marooned in our quarters.

Chapter 6
Attack!

BOOM! BOOM! BOOM!

The cannons shook the whole entire ship. It was scarier than the worst storm I ever sailed through. Inna and Gary were hiding under a blanket. And after another *BOOM* went off, I quickly climbed under the blanket with them.

"I'm right behind you," Vicky yelled, and dove headfirst next to me under the blanket.

"Arrr! You guys are a bunch of scallywags!" Aaron bellowed. He still had his face pressed up to the window. "If Rotten Tooth had taught us how to swashbuckle, I'd be up there right now."

I peeked my head out. Aaron started jumping from bunk to bunk, swinging a rope around in the air. But then a giant blast rocked the *Sea Rat* so hard that it knocked Aaron to the floor.

In a flash, he was right next to Vicky, hiding with the rest of us.

"I thought you said we were scally-wags?" Vicky asked.

Aaron shrugged his shoulders. "So, maybe I was wrong," he said. Even though Aaron liked to be a show-off, most of the time he admitted when he was wrong. This was definitely one of those times.

We could see the smoke outside our window.

We could hear the rival pirates board our ship.

We knew our ship was losing the fight.

"What are we going to do?" Vicky asked. "The crew of the *Filthy Sails* is going to take all of our treasure!"

"Arrr! They won't take my necklace," Inna said, covering it with both hands.

"Even worse, they'll sink our ship! We can't let that happen," I said. Even though

we were afraid, our ship was in danger. "We have to pull together and save the day."

"Aye aye!" Vicky said. "But what can we do?"

"We need a plan," Inna said.

"Aye, that's a good plan," Gary told her.

"Aye," Vicky agreed. "But what is the plan going to be?"

We all shrugged.

Then we thought as hard as we could.

I reached my hand under my pirate hat and scratched my head. Then I rolled my eyes back to search for a plan in my brain. That's when I remembered a story a pirate from the last ship I lived on had told me. It was about how he'd helped save that ship.

"ARRR! That's it!" I said. Then I told my friends the story about that ship being attacked. "Some of the pirates hid belowdecks in case the ship was overtaken. And then they snuck around and freed the crew. After that, *WHAM*! A surprise attack!"

"Arrr! Then what are we waiting for? Let's go, buckoes!" Aaron said.

We threw the blanket off our heads and snuck toward the door. It was up to us to save the *Sea Rat* once again.

Chapter 7
Sneaky Sea Dogs

The door creaked open. I looked around to make sure the coast was clear.

"C'mon, mates, let's go," I whispered to my friends. Then we tippy-toed through the hallway. We knew a secret way to get on deck. Down the hall was a hatch with a ladder that went up to the back of the ship. That's where we were headed.

When we got to the door, I heard a loud rumble.

I stopped dead in my tracks.

"What was that?" I whispered.

Gary looked down and put both hands on his stomach. "That was my tummy," he whispered back. "I'm starving."

"Aye, me too," Inna whispered.

"Me three," Vicky said.

Then my tummy rumbled, too.

"Lucky for you mates, I've got some sea slugs in my pocket," Aaron said. He reached into his pocket and pulled out a handful of slimy slugs.

Gary's face turned greenish. Inna held her nose. I did the same. Suddenly, we weren't so hungry anymore.

"Maybe later," we said.

"Suit yourself," Aaron said. Then he and Vicky gobbled up the creepy critters.

Once we snuck our way to the hatch, there was one little problem. The ladder wasn't there and none of us could reach the handle. "I can reach it if I climb on your shoulders," Vicky told me.

"Good idea," I said. Then Aaron helped Vicky climb on my shoulders. But we still couldn't reach. "We need someone to climb on Vicky's shoulders, too," I said.

"I vote for Gary," Inna said. Inna didn't like climbing.

"Aye!" Aaron agreed. "And we can help him."

Gary wasn't so sure. I could tell he was afraid he'd fall. "You can do it, Gary! The ship needs you," I told him.

"Aye?" Gary asked.

"AYE!" we all said.

"Then I'll try my best," he said. He took a deep breath and almost sneezed. But he pinched his nose just in time. After all, we were supposed to be sneaky.

With Aaron and Inna's help, Gary climbed on Vicky's shoulders. I felt my legs starting to shake. It was hard work holding them both.

"I got it!" Gary said when he grabbed the hatch handle. He was so excited that he lost his balance!

I wibbled and wobbled.

Then . . . *CRASH!*

I fell to the floor. Then Vicky fell on top of me. I waited for Gary to fall, but he didn't. I looked up and he was still holding onto the handle. Then the hatch started to slide open.

Gary was hanging in the air. We could

see the sky above him. "Arrr! What should I do?" he asked.

"Pull yourself up. Then lower a rope for us to climb," I said.

"Aye aye!" Gary said. We watched him disappear. When he came back, he was holding a rope.

"Use one of the knots Rotten Tooth showed us to tie the rope to the ship's railing," Inna whispered.

"Aye aye!" Gary said. The next thing we knew, he was lowering the rope down. We all took turns climbing up on deck and telling Gary what a good job he had done. Gary smiled really proudly. "I guess I'm not that clumsy when it counts," he said.

"Aye," I said, and gave him a pat on the back.

Then I looked around. We were all the way at the back of the ship, behind the main cabin. There were never any pirates here except Clegg. He was the oldest pirate on the ship, and he liked to fish back here. But I didn't even see him.

When I poked my head around the side of the cabin, I found the crew. They were tied to the masts, and the crew of the *Filthy Sails* was guarding them!

I took a deep breath. I knew I had to come up with a *really* good plan if we were going save the day once again!

Chapter 8
Rotten Luck!

I watched Captain Fish Face pace the deck. "Arrr! Tell me where be the rest of the treasure or I'll sink this *Rat* to the bottom of the sea!" he demanded. His voice was even scarier than his face. It gave me the shivers just hearing him.

We had snuck over to the far side of the ship and were hiding behind a tall stack of barrels. "We need to do something quick!" I said, peeking through the tiny space between the barrels. "Or Fish Face is going to make the crew walk the plank."

"Arrr! I say we run out there and toss Cap'n Fish Guts back into the sea," Aaron said. He stood up and was about to run out. I had to grab his sleeve to hold him back.

"There's too many of them," I said. I tried counting the pirates from the *Filthy Sails*. There were lots. I'm not sure exactly how many because I lost count at eleven. But I knew it was lots. "We need to set our shipmates free first."

"But how are we going to get to them?" Vicky asked. "They're surrounded."

Vicky was right. But no matter how hard I tried, I couldn't come up with a plan.

"Avast! I've got an idea," Inna said. "First, we need a distraction. Someone has to get those stinky pirates' attention so the rest of us can untie the crew."

Aaron jumped up. "I'll do it," he said. Then he started to swing his arms around like he was swashbuckling.

"Maybe someone else should do it," Inna said.

"Aye! Someone who isn't addled in the head," Vicky agreed.

Aaron crossed his arms. "I can do it. I'll prove it," he said.

I held up my hands. I had to stop him. They'd turn him into shark bait for sure. "Um . . . we need you to help untie the crew. You're the best at untying knots," I fibbed.

"Aye? I am, aren't I?" Aaron said. He held his chin up high. "Okay, I'll help."

I wiped my forehead. That was a close one. And for once, I didn't mind Aaron thinking he was the best at everything.

Gary tapped me on the shoulder. "Pete, I'm not very good at untying knots. But I'm very, very good at distractions," he said.

Vicky rubbed her forehead. "Aye, you can say that again," she said.

"Good! While Gary's doing that, we'll

sneak around and free Rotten Tooth," Inna said.

"Rotten Face!" Aaron moaned. "Why do you want to free him?"

"Because he's the best pirate on the ship, whether we like him or not," Inna said.

"Aye, Inna's right!" I agreed.

Then we all put our hands together and whispered our pirate cheer:

"Swashbuckling, sailing, finding treasure, too. Becoming pirates is what we want to do!"

I gave Gary a little nudge. "It's time to set sail," I said.

"Aye," Gary said. Then he started crawling to the other end of the deck. He hid behind barrels and crates until he made it all the way without anyone seeing him.

"How are we going to know when he's distracting them?" Vicky asked.

But I didn't even have to answer. Because just then, we heard a loud *AH-*

CHOO! All the pirates turned around to see where the noise came from. Then there was a big, giant *CRASH* as Gary tripped over a rope and knocked down a bunch of barrels.

"That's how!" I said. "Let's go!"

With all the pirates distracted, we rushed over to where Rotten Tooth was tied up with the rest of the crew. "Arrr! I'm glad to see you sea pups!" he said.

"Aye?" we asked.

"Aye!" Rotten Tooth said. "Untie me so

we can send Cap'n Fish Face swimming back to where he came from."

"Aye aye!" I said with a big smile. For once, Rotten Tooth was treating us like real pirates.

I hurried behind the mast. I saw the rope and found where it was tied. My mouth fell open. My eyes went all wide. "Oh no!" I told my mates. "It's a Sheepshank Man-o'-War knot!"

We all gulped! Even Rotten Tooth!

I squinted my eyes and stuck out my tongue. I was going to try my best. I just hoped all that homework was worth it.

Chapter 9
Pirate Overboard!

"Hurry, Pete!" Vicky said.

"Aye! Cap'n Fish Face has Gary!" Inna said.

"Aye, and it looks like he's going to make him walk the plank," Aaron said.

Everyone was counting on me. But no matter how I pushed or pulled, I couldn't get the knot to budge.

"Shiver me timbers, what's taking so long! Can't ye rats just chew through the rope?" Rotten Tooth growled.

Inna held her stomach and gagged. "Yuck! That slimy rope probably tastes even worse than sea slugs."

Vicky made a grumpy face. "Well it probably tastes better than icky sticky fish eggs," she huffed.

Aaron interrupted their bickering. He leaned in between them and rolled his eyes at Rotten Tooth. "Arrr! We wouldn't have to chew it if Rotten Head let us have swords," he said. "We could just cut the rope."

I didn't say anything.

I took a deep breath. Then I tried the knot again.

I wasn't going to let those mean pirates make Gary walk the plank. He was my best bunkmate!

I tried to remember what Rotten Tooth had shown us. There was a special trick to it. I had to take one loop and pull it while I pushed another. I just couldn't remember which ones. So I tried all of them.

I twisted and turned and pushed and pulled. Then I pulled and pushed and turned and twisted. And after a little more twisting, the knot started to get loose.

"That's it! You almost got it," Inna said hopefully.

"Aye, almost," I said. I still needed to push and pull some more.

"AVAST! Tiny intruders!" one of the pirates from the *Filthy Sails* shouted out.

We'd been spotted!

"Cast that wee one overboard and stop the others!" Captain Fish Face shouted.

I worked faster and the rope got looser and looser.

"Avast! You did it," Vicky said as the crew members of the *Sea Rat* wiggled free.

"Aye, and just in time, too," I said. Gary was standing on the tippy edge of the plank.

"Don't worry, I'll take care of that," Rotten Tooth said. He leaped up and made a loud roar. Then he rushed off to save Gary.

The pirates from the *Filthy Sails* were no match for Rotten Tooth. I saw him grab three of them at once and toss them overboard. Then he grabbed two more and tossed them right with the others.

Soon our shipmates were all tossing pirates overboard.

In no time, Captain Fish Face was the only mean pirate left onboard. He found himself face-to-face with Captain Stinky Beard. "I'll teach you to attack my ship," Captain Stinky Beard said.

"Aye! You show 'em, Cap'n!" we cheered.

Captain Fish Face started to back up to the plank.

That's when I saw that Gary was still standing there. I waved my pirate hat in the air to get his attention. "Ahoy, Gary!" I shouted. "Over here!"

But I was too late!

Captain Fish Face stood in Gary's way. "Arrr! Back off or I'll take this lil' shipmate with me!" he said to Captain Stinky Beard. It looked like Gary was doomed.

Inna covered up her eyes with her hands. "I can't watch," she said.

"Me neither," Vicky said, and turned away.

"Arrr! We need to save him," Aaron shouted.

I didn't say anything. I saw Gary's nose twitching, and his glasses started to slide down. I knew right away that Gary was going to save himself.

"AH-AH-AH-CHOOOOO!" Gary sneezed. He sneezed so hard that he lost his balance and slipped. He slipped right into Captain Fish Face!

Captain Fish Face wibbled and wobbled.

Then *SPLASH*!

Gary had knocked him right off the plank! I guess sometimes it's pretty lucky to be as clumsy as Gary is.

Chapter 10
Pirates at Last

"All hands man the sails," Captain Stinky Beard ordered.

The crew hurried to the mast and raised the sails. The *Sea Rat* began to creak as it gained speed. We were sailing away to safety as the soggy pirates from the *Filthy Sails* climbed back aboard their ship and headed in the other direction.

I rushed over to Gary. He stood up slowly and rubbed his head. "Did I do something wrong?" he asked once he fixed his glasses and saw everyone staring at him.

"Did you do something wrong?" I said in amazement. "Great sails! You saved the ship!"

"Aye?" Gary asked.

"AYE!" the entire crew of the *Sea Rat* shouted.

Aaron, Vicky, Inna, and I picked Gary up and put him on our shoulders. Then we carried him around the deck as the crew clapped and danced. "Three cheers for our shipmate!" we yelled.

"HIP! HIP! HOORAY!" the crew sang.

Captain Stinky Beard came over to us. We put Gary down and formed a line. I was about to give the captain a salute, but before I could . . . *he gave us a salute!*

That made us smile really, really, really wide.

"Ye brave little pirates did a fine job," Captain Stinky Beard told us. I was so happy, I wanted to sing a sea shanty, but then Captain Stinky Beard turned to Rotten Tooth. "And ye, me first mate, have done a great job, too! Not only did you fight off those pesky pirates, but your shipshape teaching saved the day!"

"Arrr! Just doing me duty," Rotten Tooth said with a smile.

That made me not so happy anymore. Rotten Tooth had only taught us the Sheepshank Man-o'-War knot to keep us out of the way. I looked at my friends, and they didn't look so happy, either.

"Arrr . . ." I started to say, but Rotten Tooth put his hand over my mouth.

"Aye, Cap'n. But I couldn't have done it without these here kiddies," he said. "They be a clever bunch of pirates."

None of us could believe our ears! Not only had Rotten Tooth said we were clever, but he hadn't even called us dogs, or pollywogs, or anything else mean. He'd called us *pirates*!

Captain Stinky Beard told us again how proud he was before he walked off to steer the ship. We all turned our heads up to look at Rotten Tooth. Our mouths were still hanging open in surprise.

"Does this mean we can learn something more fun than knots tomorrow?" I asked.

"Aye!" Rotten Tooth said.

"HOORAY!" we cheered. Then we all

danced around happily, even though it wasn't very piratey to dance.

"Tomorrow, I'll be teaching ye to stitch the sails," Rotten Tooth said with a rotten grin. We stopped dancing right away. I guess Rotten Guts hadn't completely changed his mind about us after all.